D0258631

SKELLY
the Skeleton Girl

SIMON AND SCHUSTER
First published in Great Britain in 2007 by Simon & Schuster UK Ltd
Africa House, 64-78 Kingsway, London WC2B 6AH
A CBS company

Originally published in 2007 by Simon & Schuster Books for Young Readers,
an imprint of Simon & Schuster Children's Publishing Division, New York

Copyright © 2007 by Jimmy Pickering
Book design by Lizzy Bromley
The text for this book is set in Stanyan
The art for this book was created using mixed media

The right of Jimmy Pickering to be identified as author and illustrator of this work has been
asserted in accordance with sections 77 and 78 of the Copyright, Designs and Patents Act, 1988

All rights reserved, including the right of reproduction in whole or in part in any form

A CIP catalogue record for this book is available from the British Library

ISBN -10: 1-84738-093-X
ISBN -13: 978-1-84738-093-7

Printed in Singapore
10 9 8 7 6 5 4 3 2 1

631 4123

CORK CITY LIBRARY
WITHDRAWN
FROM STOCK

To Julian Chaney, the best pal this Skeleton Boy has ever had!

SKELLY
the Skeleton Girl

Written and illustrated by
JIMMY PICKERING

SIMON AND SCHUSTER, London

My name is

SKELLY.

I'm a skeleton girl.

This is my HOUSE, high on a hill.

I found a BONE
lying on my floor.

I asked my BAT
as we went for a stroll.

"No," he said.
"Does it belong to YOU?"

Could it be a BONE from me?
No, it wasn't mine.

X-RAY

I tickled the MONSTER
under the stairs, and he
started to LAUGH.

I knew he still had
his FUNNY BONE.

I asked my
MAN-EATING plants.

"No, my dear,
we wouldn't
eat THAT!"

I asked the GHOSTS who came to tea
if it belonged to them.

"Honey, we have no BONES."
"We lost those long ago."

I asked the SPIDER
who lived next door
if it could be his.

I checked my dolls from
HEAD to TOE. . .
They hadn't lost
a STITCH.

This bony search was
making me HUNGRY.
I went to the kitchen
for a piece of CAKE.

past my
MAN-EATING plants,
into the
GARDEN.

I peeked around the **TOPIARY HEDGE** to see what the **NOISE** could be.

"Does this belong to YOU?"

I found the owner of the BONE,
and I found a new
FRIEND, too!